NEWF

Marie Killilea

ILLUSTRATED BY

Ian Schoenherr

PHILOMEL BOOKS · NEW YORK

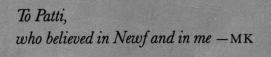

To Patti,
who believed in Newf and in me —MK

For Nyssa, Emily, Ryan, Alex, and Tess
—IS

Library of Congress Cataloging-in-Publication Data   Killilea, Marie (Marie Lyons)
Newf / by Marie Killilea : illustrated by Ian Schoenherr.   p.   cm.   Summary: A Newfoundland dog comes
mysteriously out of the sea and takes up residence with a small white kitten in a deserted cottage.   ISBN 0-399-21875-0
[1. Dogs—Fiction.   2. Cats—Fiction.]   I. Schoenherr, Ian, ill.   II. Title.   PZ7.K557Ne   1992   [E]—dc20   91-31152 CIP AC

10 9 8 7 6 5 4 3 2 1

First Impression

There was a time, long, long ago, when the cottage stood sturdy and strong on a bluff overlooking the ocean. It was a fisherman's cottage. The sea pounded the rocks below, but smoke curled from the chimney. Inside there were cupboards and shelves filled with jars of jams, and there were kerosene lamps that shed pools of golden light. The house was made merry by a mother's song and a child's laughter.

But it was a sad cottage now, for the family had left it so long ago that no one remembered why. A deserted cottage with tilting walls and a crumbling roof. The wind from the ocean roamed through the house, and the remaining bed was a nesting place for raccoons.

It was a day in spring when flower and fern began poking their heads out of the brown earth. As the sea rushed to meet the shore, a large black dog was carried by the waves up on the sand. There was no fishing boat to be seen. It was a puzzle whence he had come. The dog, a Newfoundland, rested a minute, then rose and shook himself. He clambered up over the rocks and came to the deserted cottage.

He sniffed the smells of four-legged visitors that had come before him and then was arrested by a cry: a small, weak cry.

In the corner of the room was a pile of old fisherman's netting. He lowered his massive head to it and was rewarded with a stinging slap of claws. He bolted back in surprised hurt. He moved cautiously to look again, ready to leap back.

From the coils there emerged a skinny, dirty white kitten.

He had never seen a creature like this before. The kitten crept toward him and sniffed one of the huge webbed feet. The dog lowered his head. The kitten hissed and struck again. Offended, the dog rose, turned, and went out.

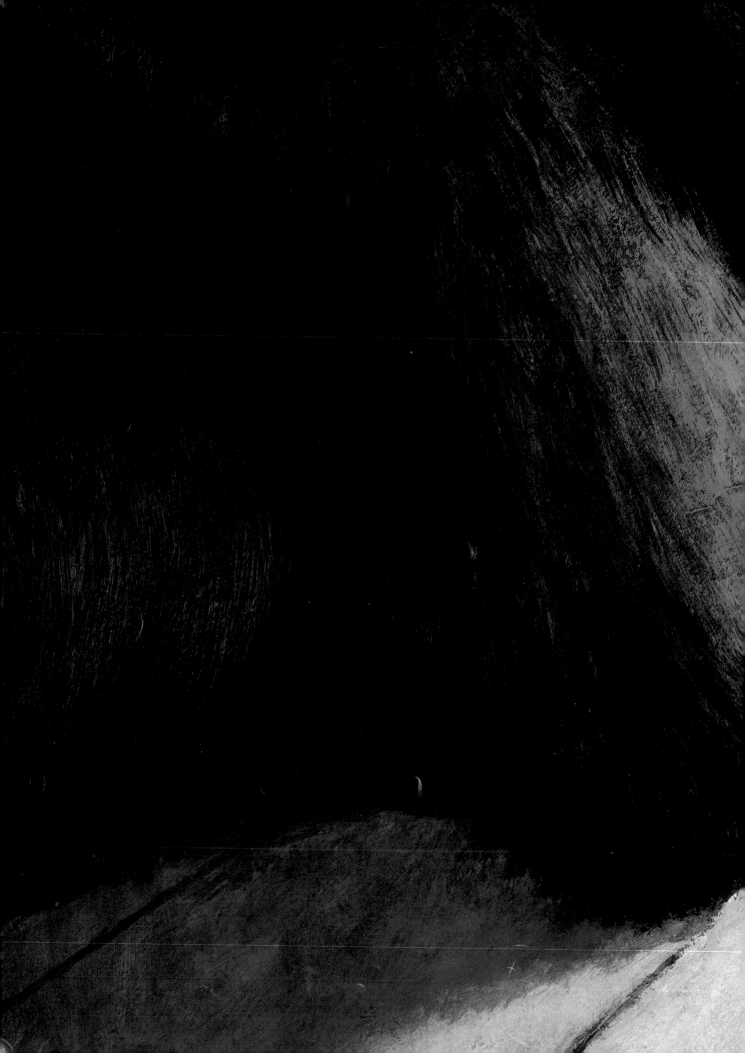

Not long after he came back with a large fish in his great
jaw. The Newf lay down and began to eat. The kitten cried
piteously. He too was hungry. Cautiously he inched closer to
share the meal, keeping a watchful eye on the Newf.
    There was enough for both. They ate their fill and slept.

Stretched out, the dog looked like a large black bear with a plumed tail. On waking, Kitten decided to investigate this strange animal. He crept closer and Newf watched him curiously. He walked around the gigantic dog, keeping a safe distance away. When the dog stirred, Kitten humped his back and hissed. Newf paid no attention. Then he wagged his tail, and Kitten pounced. The dog wagged his tail again, and again the kitten pounced. Again and again and again.

Here was an exciting game: wag, advance, pounce, retreat.

Tiring of the game, Kitten bravely moved closer to Newf's
side and went to sleep. Newf turned his head and began to lick
his companion—long swipes from head to tail. His tongue was
warm and rough as the kitten's mother's had been. Kitten liked
this washing and lay quietly until his fur was as white as snow.

Evening came, and as the moon climbed in the sky, the wolves
on the near hills began to sing. Kitten shivered and moved
to the warmth of Newf's belly. He wasn't afraid anymore.

In the morning Newf went to the beach for a swim, Kitten following close behind. With scarcely a ripple, Newf slid into the water and swam out. Kitten watched from the water's edge. When his feet got wet, he shook them.

Suddenly a rogue wave snatched Kitten from the shore and swept him out, tossing and turning him over and over. Newf saw the helpless body buffeted by the waves.

Churning effortlessly through the water, he seized his gasping friend by the neck and, lifting his head regally above the waves, carried him back to shore. Kitten coughed and shuddered, and Newf licked him all over. Finally Kitten sat up, then bounded to his feet.

The days of summer were happy days. They chased butter-flies together, and Newf nibbled berries from the vines that grew near the cottage. Kitten found a family of skunks to play with. Newf kept his distance.

During fall Newf continued to take his daily swim. Kitten stayed far away from the water. Instead of butterflies, they chased red and gold leaves, which tumbled and whispered around them. Kitten had gotten quite big on his diet of fish, mice, and an occasional mole.

Then suddenly it was winter. The raccoons again sought shelter on the bed. The wind howled around the cottage and slammed the remaining shutters against the tilting walls. Then one day snow fell, gently at first, but it continued through the night and grew heavier with each passing hour. Newf loved to sleep out in the snow but stayed in the cottage to keep Kitten closer to him and warm.

In the morning Newf made his way to the beach through the huge drifts. Kitten didn't follow.

When he returned, Newf couldn't find Kitten. He snuffled each part of the cottage, scratched at the fish net, then went outside. The snow had erased any footprints and any odor. He went to the snow-laden spots where Kitten used to hide— behind the sled, behind the oars, behind the shovel. He barked and barked again.

He tilted his head to listen. There was no sound.

His anxiety mounted, and he began to whimper and to whine. He ran from place to place around the cottage, using his muzzle as a plow through drifts of snow. His bark grew more shrill. As he raced, he sent up showers of snow but uncovered nothing. White cat in a snow storm!

He struggled through drifts to the woodpile and tore at the logs with all the power of his fear. In his onslaught he knocked over a large stack, then put all the strength of his body into dislodging what remained.

Then he heard a cry—a weak mewing suffocated by snow.

He dug above it and heard a louder cry. Front feet digging
frantically, he saw his friend entombed. He dug around him,
lowered his head, and finally lifted him out.

Kitten had grown big and heavy, but Newf's mouth was
bigger and he was powerful. His hold on Kitten was strong but
gentle. Plowing his way through drift after drift, he carried
Kitten to the cottage.

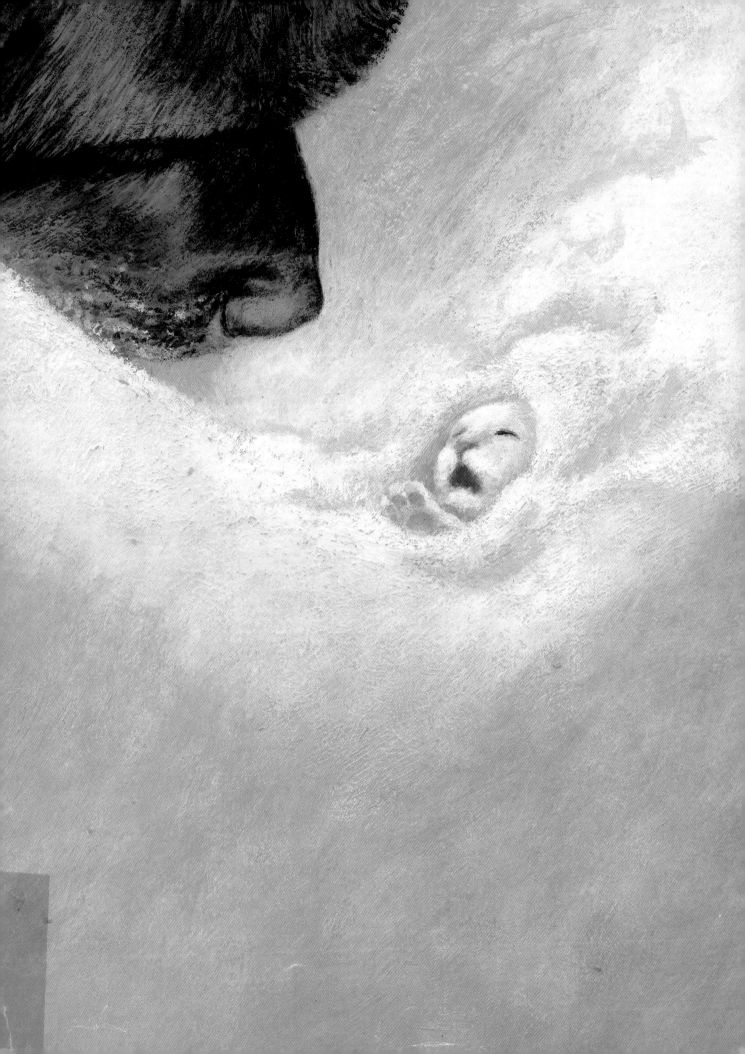

He squeezed through the doorway, put Kitten down, then lay with his forelegs wrapped around him. Kitten stopped mewing as his shivering ceased, and he snuggled into the warmth of Newf's deep barrel chest.

Newf was tired—so very tired—but he was content, and his heart swelled with happiness as a peaceful sound fell on the silence: Kitten was purring.

There was a cottage that stood sturdy and strong on a bluff overlooking the sea. It was a fisherman's cottage, but it was no longer deserted.